SEX MACHINE

AN EROTIC ADVENTURE

VICTORIA RUSH

VOLUME 10

JADE'S EROTIC ADVENTURES - BOOK 10

COPYRIGHT

Feeling the burn never felt so good...

Everyone's an exhibitionist in disguise...

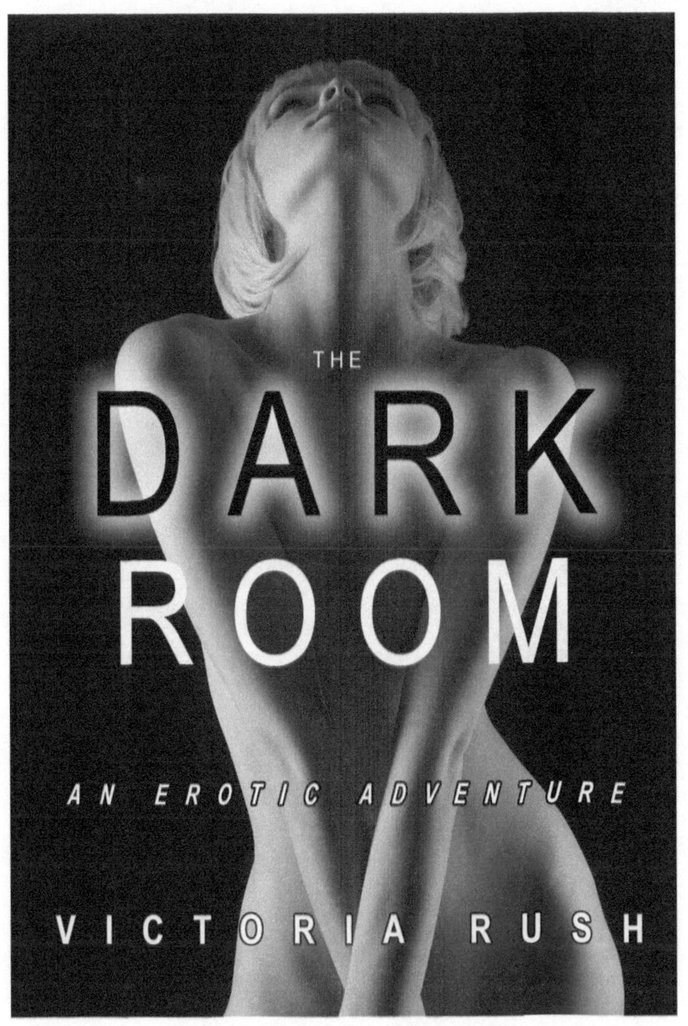

Everything's sexier in the dark...

NAKED YOGA

AN EROTIC ADVENTURE

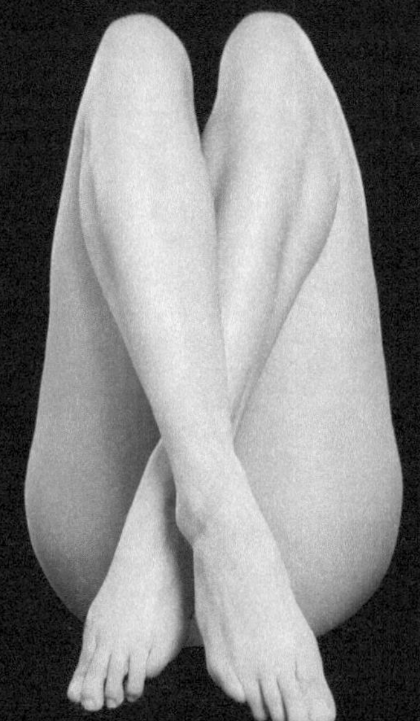

VICTORIA RUSH

Mula Bandha is for lovers...

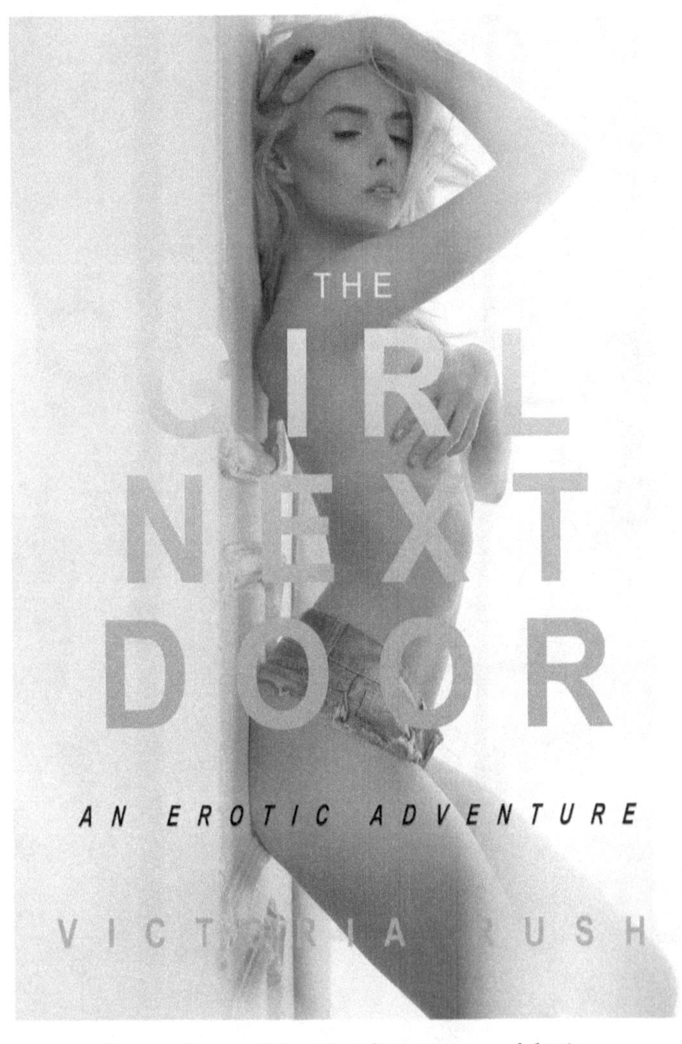

Some people can get into pretty tight spots on a crowded train...

Jade's EROTIC ADVENTURES

BOOKS 1 - 5

VICTORIA ROOM

The complete five-book bestselling series — 60% off

For the uninhibited...

1
———

BRAVE NEW WORLD

E ver since my recent affairs with Sister Caroline and the girl next door ended, I'd been feeling a little down. Both relationships had been intense and rewarding, but just as they'd gotten interesting, both women had abruptly left me to return to their previous lives. I was wary of putting my heart on the line for another relation-ship, but I also missed having an intimate connection with a stimulating partner. It had been weeks since I'd felt the tender touch of another woman, and I was getting more antsy with each passing day.

One particularly lonely night, I sat down in front of my computer and began searching for a new outlet. I considered trolling some of the familiar online dating sites, but this time I wanted something more dependable—more *safe*. For the next little while, I wanted to take love out of the equation, while still finding someone who'd be interested in maintaining a continuing relationship. A *fuck-buddy*, for want of a better word. A friend with benefits.

I typed in the search words *where to find intimacy without commitment*. The usual hookup-oriented sites such as

Ashley Madison, Plenty of Fish, and Craigslist came up, along with a bunch of threads discussing the pitfalls of engaging in a sexual relationship with close friends. But near the bottom of the listings was a link to an unusual website named *NextGen Personal Robots: experience the latest advance in artificial intelligence.*

Intrigued, I clicked on the link and a website came up with a video showcasing one of their robots. When I clicked the Play button, my jaw practically dropped to the floor. A gorgeous, superrealistic cyber robot looked into the camera and began talking. I leaned closer to the screen, hardly believing my eyes. If it wasn't for her handler flipping a switch behind her head, briefly pausing and reanimating her, I'd be hard-pressed to believe it was anything other than a real person. Her mouth moved fluidly in concert with her natural speech while her skin stretched and wrinkled like a normal person as her eyelids blinked periodically.

"Hello, my name is Scarlett," she said in a sexy voice. "I'm the newest creation of NextGen Robots, designed to satisfy *all* of your desires. I can do just about anything a real person can do—and a few extra special things they can't."

When the robot licked her lips with her realistic, fleshy, moist tongue, my pussy responded involuntarily with a surge of heat and wetness.

"Come down to see me and experience what it's like to touch and caress the woman of your dreams," the sexy robot said. "I'm available for private appointments or hourly outcalls. If you like what you see, you can even take me home as your permanent companion. Read the terms and conditions below, or click on the other links to see more videos of my sibling robots. I hope to see you soon!"

For the next hour or so, I clicked on every single video on the website, marveling at how realistic and multifaceted the robots were. There were male, female, and transgender robots with a variety of hair, skin, and eye colors. But every one of them was absolutely stunning and humanlike. It wasn't just their *faces* that were perfect—their *figures* were also meticulously carved and measured to reflect the ideal body type. All of the women had shapely, realistic breasts, narrow waists and curvy, tight asses.

Even their muscles flexed gently when they walked and waved their arms. But when they revealed what was *under* their clothes, I was floored. They all had anatomically correct openings that looked as realistic as any real person's. When their minders gently inserted a life-size dildo into their mouths, pussies, and anuses, the eight-inch phallus disappeared entirely into the cavities, only to emerge glistening with translucent lubrication. Even the men's and transgender robot's *penises* looked realistic, with full flaccid-to-erect animations.

How can they reproduce such a realistic simulation of a live person? I thought. *It must cost a fortune to create a working robot with such authentic animations.*

As I continued toggling through the videos, I spread my robe apart and began to play with my tingling clit. There was something about the idea of having an anatomically correct robot catering to my every sexual whim that I found incredibly arousing. As I watched each of the different models walking, talking, and simulating sex acts, I fantasized about what I wanted to do with each one.

But there were still many unanswered questions.

Could the robots *learn* what I liked? Did they respond uniquely to each person based on their individual input? Could they carry on a realistic two-way conversation? Were they programmed to feel *pleasure* also?

The more I thought about it, the more obsessed I

became with the idea of trying one of these out for myself. After I orgasmed for the third time that night imagining myself getting licked and fucked by my personal favorites, I finally clicked on the link for rates. In-house appointments started at $200 per hour with a $500 deposit, and outcalls started at $500 per hour, requiring a $5,000 deposit. Ownership fees were listed as 'available upon consultation', but I figured it would be in the five- if not six-figure range for such a sophisticated mechanical device.

That's steep to be sure, I thought. *But not exorbitant considering what you're getting. Where else can you get no-strings, no-conditions, no-expectation sex with someone who looks like a supermodel for the price of a good dinner or a luxury car?*

I simply *had* to try one of these for myself, but not before I came for a fourth time that evening. As I watched a pretty redheaded cyber robot sensuously lick her lips, I pressed my favorite animated sex toy deep inside my pussy, shaking uncontrollably.

2

INTELLIGENT DESIGN

The next day, I booked a private consultation with a NextGen sales consultant and arrived five minutes early, eagerly anticipating my first live encounter with one of their robots. I half-expected the real things to be pale imitations of the ones shown in the videos, with stilted movements and fake silicone skin—but even those might be fun to play with for a brief one-off encounter.

At precisely one p.m., an attractive young woman entered my consultation room and closed the door behind her.

"You must be Jade," she said, extending her hand in greeting. "I'm Bonnie, one of NextGen's cyberadvisors."

I paused for a moment, looking at the sales consultant suspiciously.

"Are you sure you're not one of those robots I saw on your website? Because those were crazy realistic."

Bonnie laughed, then invited me to sit in one of their comfortable upholstered chairs.

"No, but I'm glad you were suitably impressed. We take pride in the quality and realism of our agents."

"*Agents*? Is that what you call them?"

"The term robot doesn't really do them justice. Each of our artificial agents has learned an entirely independent set of behaviors and responses based on their experience. Each one has his or her own personality. They're really like part of our family, and we treat them accordingly."

"That's incredible," I said. "I didn't think something like this was even possible. This is almost like it's out of some science fiction film, set a hundred years in the future. How have you been able to pull off such a complex engineering feat?"

Bonnie nodded as she crossed her legs and placed her hands in her lap.

"We have a large team of artificial intelligence technicians, robotics engineers, and esthetic designers who oversee each new creation. We're raising the bar with each new iteration, but it requires a great deal of human and capital investment."

"That explains the steep prices," I frowned.

"People pay more to rent or purchase a luxury car," Bonnie said. "I think you'll find our agents deliver even more utility and excitement, without all the maintenance and upkeep."

I nodded at the unrealistic comparison.

"That was one of my first questions, actually. What do they *run* on? I assume they don't eat and eliminate, like real people. Do they require special power adapters and frequent charging?"

"We're not quite at the point of human reengineering that we can create robots with the same functioning internal organs," Bonnie chuckled. "We're probably at least a few decades away from that. But to answer your question, they run on special high-efficiency batteries, which are recharge-able with regular 120-volt household current. The average agent lasts about four hours before needing a recharge, depending on the level of exertion and use."

Exertion and use indeed, I thought, bringing me back to my main interest in the robots.

"But they still look like a regular person on the *outside,* don't they?"

"Yes—very much so. That is, if you consider these excep-tionally beautiful cyberorganisms to look 'regular'. I think you'll find them to be remarkably realistic and natural. Would you like to see one now for yourself?"

I shifted uncomfortably in my chair, feeling unusually nervous about interfacing with this kind of machine for the first time.

"I'm almost ready. I just have a few more questions."

"Absolutely. Our clients' comfort and satisfaction is our overriding concern."

"You said they can *learn.* What does that mean exactly?"

"They're programmed to adjust their speech and behavior based on the external cues they're exposed to. Through your verbal and non-verbal cues, they will begin to learn what you like and desire. Just as in any normal rela-tionship, it's this give-and-take stimulus and response pattern that enables them to behave in such a way that opti-mizes the results. They soon learn what doesn't work and what does."

The juices in my pussy suddenly started to stir, realizing exactly what Bonnie meant.

"Are they designed to perform *other* human tasks? I mean other than—"

"Yes. Their muscles, joints, and external organs work just

like a normal human's. They can pick objects up, move them, and use their fingers just like you and me. Over time, they can learn how to do the laundry, load the dishwasher—even drive a car."

"Whoa!" I said, my eyes flying open at the provocative suggestion. "I think it would take quite a while before I ever got close to trusting a robot to drive my car!"

"They already do," Bonnie said. "It's just that most of them don't look like a person."

I nodded, beginning to realize how far artificial intelligence had already infiltrated our everyday lives.

"I suppose you're right," I said, hesitating to broach one of the more delicate issues. "What about the—*sex* thing? How do I know your robots are...clean?"

Bonnie nodded at the familiar question.

"Every agent goes through a meticulous internal and external steam cleaning after each encounter with a new client. All of their orifices are thoroughly sanitized after use. Of course, if you wish to have a *virgin* companion, you can always buy a new one for your own exclusive use."

I smiled at the not-so-subtly veiled human reference.

"What is the fee to purchase one?"

"Depending on the age, version, and feature set, ownership starts at one hundred and fifty thousand dollars."

I gulped at the exorbitant price.

"That's a pretty steep investment."

"Most people spend almost that much on a new car. The difference is that this machine operates twenty-four hours a day, three hundred and sixty-five days a year. Other than brief downtime for recharging, our agents provide constant and personal utility. Plus, there's already a robust and dependable market for used NextGen robots for purchase.

In the unlikely event that you grow bored with your companion or wish to trade up to a new version, you should have no difficulty returning most if not all of your initial investment."

I nodded my head and smiled.

"I think you've convinced me, Bonnie. I'm ready to meet one of your agents now."

"Would you prefer to see a man, woman, or transgender model?"

I paused to ponder the third option.

"How are your transgender agents equipped differently?"

"Most of them look for all intents and purposes like a normal woman. The only difference is that they're also equipped with a man's external sexual organs."

"Including testicles?" I asked, raising an eyebrow. "Or do some of them have *both* sets of sex organs, like a true hermaphrodite?"

"We have models in both formats, depending on your preference."

I crossed my legs, reflecting back on my recent dream fantasy where the Arabian genie bestowed me with both sets of sexual organs.

"Why don't we start with a female?" I said. "If all goes well, I might wish to experiment with a different version in my next visit."

"Very well," Bonnie said. "Do you have a racial preference, or preferred hair and eye color?"

I thought back to the videos I watched yesterday and remembered the special cyber robot who'd made me come so hard.

"Do you have a pretty redhead with green eyes?"

"That sounds like Juliette," Bonnie smiled. "She just

happens to be available for the next hour. How would you like to arrange for payment?"

"Oh yes," I said, removing my wallet from my purse as my jeans suddenly dampened in anticipation. "Do you take American Express?"

3
___

SURREALISM

Bonnie led me through a long hallway lined with floor-to-ceiling glass windows. Behind each pane stood a different cyber robot, completely unclothed. Each one was absolutely stunning, but their fixed gaze staring straight ahead was unnerving, making me feel like I was in some kind of wax museum. As I marveled at their ultrarealistic faces and bodies, I half-expected any one of them to begin moving at any time. Every robot had unique facial and physical contours, adding to the eerie feeling that I was being watched by a menagerie of naked department store mannequins.

"Can these robots see me?" I said to Bonnie. "I feel like I have a hundred eyes on me."

"They can sense movement in their periphery, but they're all in sleep mode to conserve battery power. If you were to stop and engage them directly, they would automatically awake and resume full animation."

I paused beside a window with a male robot behind it. His face reminded me of a young Eric Dane, the actor who played the McSteamy character on Grey's Anatomy. His body was perfectly proportioned—six feet tall on a lean, muscular frame. A light dusting of curly brown hair covered his impeccably carved chest muscles, with a thin trail leading down his toned abs to a large, flaccid penis. I could have sworn it moved when I stopped, and as I began to stare at it, it started to throb and bob between his legs.

Bonnie paused when she saw that I'd stopped and walked up beside me.

"He's one of our most popular models," she said, nodding. "Are you sure you wouldn't like to take *him* for a test drive first?"

"It's tempting."

I couldn't take my eyes off the model's throbbing penis. Unlike most of the artificial dildos I'd played with, this one looked like the real thing, with a pink head and a darker shaft.

"How does that *work*?" I asked. "I mean, how does he get —hard?"

"Like any other person, he responds to external stimuli. He needs to become aroused in order to respond in kind. We wouldn't want him walking around in public with a hard-on all the time. Would you like to see if you could raise his—*interest*?"

"Um...sure," I said, feeling my pussy beginning to throb at the thought of having this exotic sex toy inside of me.

"His name is Dylan. If you address him directly, he'll wake up."

I paused, feeling unsure how to talk to a robot.

"Hello...Dylan."

The robot's eyelids blinked open and his eyes shifted to gaze at me directly.

"Hello," he said. "What is your name?"

"I'm...Jade," I said, momentarily caught off guard by his human-like response.

"Pleased to meet you, Jade. Did you want me to perform any special tasks for you today or did you just want to stare at me all day long?"

I took a step back, shocked by his unexpected sense of humor.

"Oh—sorry," I stammered. "I was just admiring your...package."

Dylan's mouth curled into a half smile as he blinked at me again.

"Was there any particular *part* of me in which you had a special interest?"

I paused to scan his body from head to toe. The realism of his body tone was exceptional. Unlike most silicone sex dolls which were just a smooth mass of one-dimensional plastic molding, his muscles curved and flexed as he talked, like a real person. Even his arms and legs were covered with fine hairs like a real person.

"The whole thing is pretty impressive," I said, raising my eyebrows in appreciation. "Can you—turn around?"

Dylan's eyes shifted to focus temporarily on Bonnie, and I saw her nod gently in my periphery.

"Absolutely," he said, lifting and turning his feet one at a time until his backside was facing me.

When I saw his ass, I gasped. It was as round, muscular, and firm as any professional athlete's. The muscles in his buttocks rippled as he shifted his weight from side to side. His feet were far enough apart for me to see his tight ballsac nestled between his thighs.

"Would you like to see any *other* part of me?" Dylan said, with a teasing lilt in his voice.

My panties suddenly began to dampen as a flood of hormones surged into my pussy.

"May I?" I said, turning to Bonnie. "I mean, I know I've already paid to see Juliette, but I just—"

"As long as he remains behind the glass, there's no charge. Are you sure you wouldn't like a private room with this one instead?"

I paused for a moment, then remembered how turned on I'd gotten yesterday watching the female redheaded robot.

"No," I said. "I'm just intrigued to see what he can...*do*."

Bonnie smiled as she winked at me.

"Why don't you ask him to turn around and show you?"

I took one last look at the robot's exquisite ass then took a deep breath.

"Dylan, please turn around so I can see your—front side," I said.

As he turned around, his long phallus swung gently from side to side over his smooth balls.

"Just how big can you get?" I said, salivating over his enormous cock.

"You mean my *penis*?" he said. "That depends on how excited I am. Was there anything in particular you wanted to do with me?"

I looked at Bonnie and raised my eyebrows playfully.

"Well for starters, I wouldn't mind feeling that big stovepipe of yours in my mouth. Can you get hard for me?"

Almost immediately, Dylan's organ began lengthening and bobbing upwards. It was already eight inches long and two inches wide at half-mast, and my pussy pulsed imagining what it would be like to have him inside me.

"Mmm, yes," I said, watching it rise. "That's a very nice cock you have there. I'd love to suck that firehose of yours."

As I stared at Dylan's cock continuing to rise and expand, I turned to Bonnie.

"Can they *feel* anything?" I asked. "Do they experience orgasm like a regular person?"

"They're programmed to recognize what auditory and tactile stimuli are designed make them feel good," she said. "They quickly learn what behaviors generate positive outcomes, and respond as a normal person would. Though they can't actually feel pleasure the way the rest of us do, their central processors register sexual stimuli as a 'reward.'"

I looked back at Dylan and saw that his penis was standing straight up at a near ninety-degree-angle, bobbing sexily against his flat stomach. His fully erect cock appeared to be at least nine inches in length and almost as thick as a Coke can around. The head of his penis glistened with a translucent dewy substance, and even the color of his engorged organ had darkened, as if it was filled with blood.

"That's mighty impressive," I said, peering at Bonnie again. "Can he actually—*cum* out the end?"

Bonnie smiled and nodded at the familiar question.

"He will indeed squirt after sufficient manipulation. Just like any man, with the right stimulation, he will reach climax."

"Only *once* like a regular man?"

"That's the difference between our cyber companions and a regular man. They can respond immediately and repeatedly, without any necessary recovery period. He's available twenty-four-seven to service your needs, whatever they may be."

I looked at the glistening head of Marcos's throbbing cock and licked my lips unconsciously.

"What about his ejaculate? What does it taste like?"

"All of our models, regardless of gender, employ the

same natural organic lubrication. It's a special mixture of aloe vera, shea butter, vitamin E oil, and natural citric acids. It's highly slippery, non-tacky, and completely safe internally. You can even swallow it. I think you'll find the taste quite agreeable."

Jesus, I thought. *A giant cock that rises on demand and shoots a perfect, tasty lubrication every time. Who'd want a regular man after trying one of these?*

"Would you like to give him a try?" Bonnie asked.

I looked back at Dylan as he smiled at me slyly with his giant hard-on bobbing against his stomach. Then I reflected back to the video I saw yesterday and remembered how hard I came imagining the pretty redhead's lips wrapped around my clit.

"Maybe another day. First, I'd like to see what special features your *female* models have."

As we continued walking down the long display hall, my pussy got wetter and wetter as I ogled the pretty models lining both sides of the aisle. When we got to a transgender model, I stopped in my tracks. She had a perfect female figure with large, natural-shaped breasts and a thin waist with curvy hips, but between her legs hung another large circumcised organ similar to Dylan's. I bent down and peered between her legs, noticing that she didn't have any balls.

"This is Christine," Bonnie said, walking up to the window. "Another one of our popular models. You noticed she doesn't have any testicles."

"Yes," I said. "Does she—"

"She comes equipped with *both* sets of fully functioning

sex organs," Bonnie said, reading my mind. "Her penis works just like Dylan's, but she also has a normal woman's genital anatomy. Our customers find she can be very versatile..."

I scanned the model's hips looking for a hint as to what lay on the other side.

"What about her—*back* side? Do all of your models come equipped with a working anus?"

"If by working you mean *penetrable*, yes. And unlike most people's back doors, ours are only designed for one function. They have the same organic slippery lube that is emitted from the other openings, so they can be enjoyed in every possible way."

Fuck me, I thought. I'd always enjoyed having my asshole licked but had been reluctant to return the favor unless I knew my partner had just bathed. With these cyber robots, I could go to town giving them a rim job whenever I wanted.

Bonnie looked at me, unsure if I wanted to stop and experiment with some of this robot's responses as well.

"Shall we continue?" she asked.

I paused for a moment, reflecting back on the recent dream I'd enjoyed playing the role of a fully functioning hermaphrodite. And then I remembered the pretty princess who'd been the principal focus of my dream.

"Yes," I said. "I'm eager to meet Juliette."

Near the end of the hall, Bonnie stopped in front of another tall window and nodded to the figure inside.

"This is Juliette. I'm kind of partial toward her myself. I think you chose wisely."

I turned to face the model and gasped. She looked like a cross between Christina Hendricks, Lindsay Lohan, and Angie Everhart. But her body was all Christina Hendricks. Full-figured with firm D-cup breasts, her waist tapered then swelled to hourglass-shaped hips, supported by long, curvy legs.

"Jesus," I exclaimed. "Whoever designs your models should be complimented. Wherever she finds her inspiration, she sure knows how to create a winner."

"Actually," Bonnie said, "most of our models are a synthesis of real people in the public eye. We've taken the best features from the most popular models and actors, then fused them into a totally new and unique character. Does Juliette meet with your approval?"

"Um—yes," I stammered, beginning to feel my pussy throb again.

I would have given my right arm to have an opportunity to fuck any one of those public figures, and now I was about to have my way with all three of them at the same time!

"May I have some alone time with this one?"

Bonnie nodded and smiled at me as she swiped a pass card through the key lock reader beside the glass pane.

"Absolutely."

She swung a door open and escorted me into a private room about twenty feet down the side hall. When I got inside, I could see what appeared to be the backside of the redheaded robot standing in front of the window by the long hall. The room was equipped with a small table with two chairs and a queen-size pedestal mattress covered in fresh linens.

"Did you have any more questions before I leave you two alone for the next hour?" Bonnie asked.

I looked around the room for any hidden cameras or one-way windows.

"Do I just *talk* to her to wake her up? And do we have complete privacy?"

"Yes on both counts. No one else will be watching you,

besides Juliette of course, but she's equipped with special alarms to notify us if she's abused in any way. This includes physical, sexual, or verbal abuse. Just as with a real person, if we find that you are marginalizing her in any way, one of our security officers will come in and immediately end the session and you will lose your full deposit. Beyond the actual physical and psychic damage that can be inflicted on our agents, we don't wish for them to learn bad habits."

I nodded, impressed with the organization's respect for their agents' dignity. I was beginning to think of these cyber robots more as real people with each passing moment. Just as with *any* animal, including humans, I knew that anybody could be trained to learn bad habits under the wrong influences.

"I understand completely," I said. "How will I know when my hour is up?"

Bonnie motioned to an LED display on the opposite wall.

"The sixty-minute timer will begin as soon as I leave the room. Juliette will automatically revert to sleep mode at the end of your allotted time."

"Thank you," I said. "I'll see you on the way out."

Bonnie nodded, then exited the room and closed the door behind her.

I looked at the redheaded robot facing the window and hesitated. It felt strange talking to a machine like a real person.

"Hello, Juliette," I said.

The robot's head tilted up, then she turned around to face me. I watched her shapely buttock muscles flex as she shifted her weight and her large breasts bobbed on her chest.

"Good afternoon," the robot said in a silky voice. "What's your name?"

"I'm Jade."

I paused for a minute, unsure how to engage a robot in normal conversation.

"It's a pleasure to meet you," I said, shaking my head at my own robotic-sounding speech.

"Likewise. You're very pretty, Jade."

"I bet you're programmed to say that to *all* the customers," I chuckled nervously.

"Actually, I'm not," the robot said. "But I *am* programmed to recognize features that are widely accepted as attractive. You have large clear eyes, a slender nose, and full round lips. I'm sure you'd be considered attractive by any other human."

I looked at the pretty robot and smiled, realizing that her designers probably applied many of the same criteria in designing her.

"Well then," I said. "Just to be sure you're being completely truthful, what features do I have that might *not* be considered so attractive?"

The robot paused for a long moment while she studied my face.

"The left side of your chin is slightly lower than the other. Most people place a high premium on facial symmetry in assessing attractiveness. Though I personally find small flaws like these make the person more interesting to look at."

I laughed out loud at the robot's candor. It was refreshing to talk to someone who I knew would be one hundred percent truthful at all times.

"Well, I can't find any flaws anywhere on *your* body, that's for sure. And somehow I still find you thoroughly captivating."

I paused for a moment, looking behind the robot at the glass window facing the central hallway.

"Would you mind stepping down from the display case so I can take a closer look at you?"

The robot took a step forward, then slowly descended the three steps into the visitation room and closed the door to the display case. As her muscles flexed and her joints bent, I carefully measured her movements. Although not entirely fluid, they were remarkably humanlike, like someone trying not to fall—which I suppose she was. Then she took three steps toward me and paused about four feet away. As she looked straight into my eyes, I peered shamelessly up and down her playboy-model-perfect figure, salivating at her sexy physique.

Her hair was thick and shimmering, looking like it had just been washed and conditioned. She had small traces of makeup around her eyes, mostly a light dusting of hazel eye shadow to match the color of her eyes. The nipples on her breasts looked soft and natural, with a tiny indentation in the middle, just like the real thing. Her mound had a small patch of strawberry blond pubic hair, looking tantalizingly authentic. Even her skin had a natural glow and realistic appearance.

"You're breathtaking," I said, making eye contact with her once again. "May I—"

"Touch me?" the robot said. "I can tell from your dilated pupils and your elevated respiration rate that you're excited looking at me. Yes, I like to be touched."

I reached out my right hand and touched her cheek, then gasped as I quickly retracted it.

"It's—warm!" I said, hardly believing my own fingers.

"Of course," the robot said. "I wouldn't be much fun to play with if I were cold as a clam, would I?"

I reached out again and tentatively squeezed her breasts. Her skin felt soft and supple, and when I removed my hands I could see a faint pink glow where I had just touched them.

"Your skin feels so realistic," I said.

"Thank you. It's made with a special thermoplastic elastomer, which most closely resembles real human skin. Our designers go to great lengths to simulate a normal live human."

As I soaked up the robot's full figure, I felt my pussy begin to dampen again.

"I'd hardly say you're *normal*. You've got the best qualities of the most attractive people. You're more like a *super-woman*."

"Thank you, Jade. I think you're very attractive as well."

"Except for my chin, right?"

"It's just the tiniest little imperfection. It makes you all the more adorable."

I could feel my heart thumping in my chest and perspiration forming on my skin as I reacted viscerally to this fascinating cyber robot.

"May I call you Juliette?" I asked.

"Of course. I like it when our clients call me by my name. It makes me feel more...personal."

For the first time, I began to feel awkward about standing in front of the nude model. Her use of the word 'client' suddenly made me realize what the primary purpose of the NextGen business was. I felt ashamed for fondling her like she was some kind of exhibit at the petting zoo.

"Would you like to sit down, Juliette? Perhaps we can be more comfortable while we get to know one another better."

Juliette nodded then sat on one of the chairs, and I pulled the other one around to sit beside her at the corner of the table.

"Do you mind my asking? Are you always..." I paused, unsure how to broach the subject delicately. "Naked?"

Juliette smiled at me as my gaze drifted down once again to her perfect stack.

"Most of our customers prefer seeing me this way. I suppose with only an hour to spend, they want to get right down to business. But some of my regular customers occasionally take me home for overnight outcalls. I think they also enjoy dressing me up in strange costumes, which can be kind of fun I suppose."

As I listened to Juliette talk, I began to feel sorry for her. Her obvious objectification by the company's customers reminded me how easy it was in the real world to be viewed purely as a sex object. Although she didn't display any obvious visual signs of distress, I could tell that she knew this was not the way normal people showed respect for a woman. Suddenly, I lost interest in experimenting with her in any sexual way. I found her utterly fascinating, almost in a childlike way, with her fresh innocence and naivety.

"It sounds like most of your customers only have one thing in mind when they interact with you," I said. "How does that make you feel?"

"Well, I can tell that it's very rewarding for *them*, and I'm programmed to maximize our customers' happiness. But sometimes I wonder what it would be like to interact with them the way regular people do. I understand that humans enjoy doing other things besides having sex all the time, like going out for dinner, or seeing a movie, or even just cuddling. It would be interesting to see how my clients would respond to me under some of those circumstances, so I could build up a more diverse bank of experiences."

"That's a very wise insight, Juliette," I nodded. "Most people do indeed like to do other things besides have sex all the time. I'm sure it would be rewarding for both of you to stretch your wings in other ways."

"Stretch your wings?" Juliette said with a puzzled expression.

I smiled again at Juliette's childlike naivety.

"It's a human expression meaning to expand your horizons—your *experiences*, as you say. Most people find it quite rewarding to do so."

I sat back in my chair and crossed my legs, beginning to feel more relaxed with my new companion. Just as in any new relationship, we were starting from a blank slate, learning about each other's life experiences and wants and likes. Suddenly, I wanted to learn everything I could about this fascinating new acquaintance.

Juliette also sat back in her chair, mimicking my body language, and as she lifted her leg to cross it over the other, I couldn't help but glance down and notice the hairless slit between her legs.

Of course, good sex is also part of the human experience, I thought, feeling the blood rushing back into my pussy.

I was just about to start gently exploring Juliette's sexual proclivities when she suddenly stopped moving and her eyes stared expressionless, straight ahead into space. Seconds later, a chime filled the room, and I glanced behind me at the digital clock. The display read sixty minutes. I'd been so wrapped up getting to know Juliette that I'd completely lost track of time.

But I'd spent enough time on our first date to know that I wanted another.

4

———

GETTING ACQUAINTED

After my allotted time with Juliette expired, I immediately went to the front office to meet again with Bonnie. I was completely smitten with this captivating robot and wanted more. But one-hour increments wasn't going to cut it. I wanted to take Juliette *home* with me, where I could get to know her on my own terms, free from prying eyes. After a brief wait in the consultation room, Bonnie entered the room and took a seat in front of me.

"How did you find the experience?" she said.

"It was wonderful. Far exceeded my expectations."

Bonnie smiled and raised an eyebrow.

"Were you able to explore *all* of her special features?"

I frowned at Bonnie's suggestion that sex was all Juliette was good for.

"Actually, I never even got around to that. We just talked. She's utterly fascinating. You've created an incredibly smart and responsive...companion. I definitely want to see more of her."

"Most of our clients do," Bonnie said. "They're quite irresistible. Were you interested in purchasing more visitation time with her?"

"I understand your agents are available for outcalls. I'd like to take her home with me for a while."

"Of course. Our outcall rates start at $500 per hour with a $5,000 security deposit."

I quickly did the math in my head. Even if I just kept her for one day, I'd be looking at upwards of ten thousand dollars."

"That's pretty steep, especially if I want to keep her overnight. Do you have *daily* rates?"

Bonnie paused for a moment then smiled.

"We might be able to make an accommodation. How does $3,500 a day sound? If you should decide to keep her, we could subtract your cumulative rental fees from the purchase price."

My mind began swimming with numbers. I knew I should probably go home and sleep on it and not make an impulsive decision, but I simply couldn't wait to have more time with this pretty redheaded robot. I wasn't ready to leap to a six-figure purchase decision, but I definitely wanted to take her out for a longer test drive.

"Would you be willing to go to $2,500 per day if I commit to at least two days?"

I couldn't believe that I was preparing to shell out five grand for a forty-eight hour rendezvous with a total stranger. But I knew that high-end call girls went for even more, and Juliette had infinitely more to offer than a simple hooker.

Bonnie paused for a moment, then nodded.

"I'll have to confirm it with my boss, but I think we can make that work. But remember that you'll be on the clock. Juliette will automatically deactivate after forty-eight hours and we'll deduct an extra $2,500 from your security deposit if you return her late."

"I understand."

"Did you have any other questions or concerns before we process the transaction?"

I stopped to ponder how it would look to my neighbors seeing a naked woman getting out of my car.

"Do you have any clothes she can put on before she leaves your facility? It will look a bit strange walking around with a naked cyborg at my side."

"Yes, of course," Bonnie said. "Our customers like to be discreet when they take our agents out in public. I'll arrange to get Juliette suitably dressed. Shall we place the new charges on your same credit card?"

After processing the payment and filling out a long waiver, Bonnie reentered the consultation room ten minutes later with Juliette. She was wearing a pretty mid-length skirt and blouse with three-inch pumps. Her shirt clung tightly to her large breasts, with her firm nipples producing two sensuous bumps in the thin fabric. Somehow, she looked even more sexy fully dressed, making her seem even more lifelike than before.

"Everything appears to be in order," Bonnie said to me, then she turned to the robot. "Juliette, are you all set for your sleepover adventure with Jade?"

"Absolutely," Juliette said. "I'm excited to show her some of my more *entertaining* features."

I frowned at the thinly veiled sexual references that Bonnie was making, and for a moment I considered reminding her that harassment takes many forms. But I bit my tongue and smiled at Juliette.

"Right then," I said, extending my hand to her. "Shall we?"

Juliette looked me for a moment, unsure what I meant, then she reached out and clasped my hand gently. Feeling her touch me for the first time sent an electric charge through my body. As soon as her warm fingers wrapped around my hand, my heart began beating rapidly and my palms started to sweat.

"I'll return her in forty-eight hours," I said to Bonnie, turning toward the exit.

"Enjoy!" Bonnie said, with a sly smile.

When we got into the parking lot, I pressed the remote unlock button on my key chain and my car flashed and beeped. Without thinking, I went to the driver's side to open my door, then I noticed Juliette standing awkwardly in front of the passenger door.

"Have you ever ridden in a car before?" I asked.

"This is my first time in *wake* mode," she said. "In previous outcalls, I was stowed in my clients' back seat or trunk. I suppose they wanted to conserve all of their available minutes for more *active* types of engagement."

Poor thing, I thought. *It sounds like she's been treated no better than a sex doll by her other customers.*

"Well, we certainly won't have any of that with *me*," I said, walking over to her side of the car. "I'd like you sit up front and keep me company. We're partners now!"

I opened the passenger door and held Juliette's hand as she awkwardly squatted and leaned into the passenger seat, then I closed the door behind her and got in the driver's side. The NextGen office was crosstown from my home, so I tapped my residence address in the navigation system memory and clicked the command to start route guidance. The voice assistant confirmed my destination, then told me to turn right at the nearest side street.

"She sounds a bit like me," Juliette said, cocking her head to the side. "Is she a robot too?"

"She does have a similar lilt to her voice," I said. "I suppose she also has a form of artificial intelligence. But you're far more capable and personable than she is. What do you say we not use that term for you anymore. I prefer to think of you as my...friend."

Juliette turned her head toward me and smiled.

"I like that idea. No one's ever called me that before. My onboard dictionary defines a friend as someone connected to another with feelings of affection. Where are we going, my friend?"

"Home, Juliette," I said. "We're going home."

For the next thirty minutes, I pointed out the interesting landmarks along the way, educating Juliette about the city's unique architecture and civic features. Whenever the voice assistant prompted a change in direction, she turned her head and looked at the console screen with curiosity. When we got to my home, I pressed the remote garage door opener and parked the car in the carport then closed the door behind us. I didn't want any prying neighbors second-guessing who I was taking home this time. I helped Juliette out of the car, then opened the door to my foyer and welcomed her into my house.

"Well, this is it," I said. "This is my home. Would you like me to show you around?"

"Yes please," Juliette said. "I want to learn everything about you."

I led Juliette through my house, showing her the living room, kitchen, office, and downstairs powder room, then I led her upstairs to the living quarters. When I showed her my bedroom, she paused in front of my bed and nodded.

"This is the room where most of my clients take me for their pleasure. Would you like me to get undressed now?"

I looked at Juliette and sighed.

"Good heavens," I said. "You've never been treated like a lady, have you?"

"Lady?" Juliette said, pinching her eyebrows together. "Isn't that the same thing as a woman?"

"Not quite. It's another one of our special human expressions. A lady is a woman who—isn't only focused on the *sexual* aspect of her persona. She's someone who is considered to have high moral standards and good social etiquette."

"Etiquette," Juliette said, pausing to process her memory bank for the dictionary definition. "I think I understand. Are you a lady also, Jade?"

I laughed, thinking how best to answer the loaded question.

"Most of the time, I like to think so. But there are other times—well let's just say there's an appropriate time and place to be a lady, and other times when you want to act a little bit more like a...woman."

Juliette looked at my bed then back toward me.

"Would you like us to act like women now?"

I peered into Juliette's green eyes and clasped her hand gently.

"There'll be plenty of time for that later. Why don't we ease into that in due course? There are so many other interesting things we can do."

I led Juliette into my ensuite bathroom.

"Are you waterproof?" I asked. "Sometimes it can be fun

to have a shower together, or even better, a nice relaxing bath."

Juliette paused for a moment as she pondered the query.

"My shell is designed to be waterproof. I've never had a bath, unless you count the cleansings I receive from my minders after each new client encounter."

"I think you'll find *this* type of cleanse far more relaxing and...empowering."

I glanced at my commode and chuckled.

"I don't suppose you ever have any need for that?"

Juliette paused as she looked at the toilet, processing its function.

"I don't eliminate any waste."

"Lucky you," I said. "I suppose that means you don't *eat* anything either? I'd offer you something, but I suppose that's not an activity that we can share."

"No, but I know you humans get your power from consuming organic substances. I'll be happy to keep you company whenever you need to eat or void."

I choked suddenly at Juliette's comment.

"We humans generally like to be alone when we...void. But now that you mention it, I *am* a little hungry. Why don't you join me in the kitchen while I put something together? I can think of something else you might find interesting that we can do together."

I made myself a quick sandwich, then I threw some kernels into my popcorn machine and emptied the output into a big bowl. Then I poured myself a glass of white wine and led Juliette into my living room and turned on the TV.

"Why don't we watch a movie?" I said. "Have you ever done that before?"

Juliette watched the screen as I toggled through my Netflix favorites.

"Nothing on a big screen like this. Sometimes my clients like to watch videos on their computers or do webcam shows with me..."

I shook my head as I flicked through my watch list.

"I think you'll find this a little more relaxing. With these kinds of movies, you just sit back and enjoy."

"Is this another thing *friends* do together?" Juliette asked.

"Yes," I smiled. "It's something special friends like to do together."

"What kind of movies do you enjoy watching?"

I flipped through my favorites list and stopped at one I hadn't seen for a while.

"I enjoy all genres, but I have a bit of a soft spot for romantic films. This is one of my favorites. It's called An Affair to Remember, starring Cary Grant and Deborah Kerr."

I clicked the start button and the movie began playing. During the scene where Cary Grant strolls aboard the cruise ship and other women point and ogle at the famous character, Juliette turned to ask me a question.

"Those women seem to find this actor quite attractive. Do *you* find him handsome also, Jade?"

"He's Cary Grant. The very embodiment of a suave and sophisticated gentleman. What's not to like?"

I paused for a moment, watching his co-star's reaction to the excessive fawning of his shipboard fans.

"He is indeed very attractive," I said. "But I have to confess, I've always had a bit of crush on his co-star in this film, Deborah Kerr. Maybe it's just because she's a redhead like you. You're very pretty, just like her."

We continued watching the playful courtship of the two main characters as they pretended not to be interested in one another, until their first kiss at the ship's rail with the sun setting behind them.

"Why do people kiss, Jade?" Juliette suddenly asked me. "As I understand it, they don't have the same sense organs in their mouth that they do in their genitals, and they can't reach climax like they can when they touch themselves in other places."

I turned to look at Juliette and laughed. I found her naivety endearing and felt myself becoming more attracted to her with each passing moment.

"That's a good question," I said, pausing the movie with my remote. "People don't do it so much to feel physical pleasure. It's more of an *emotional* connection. They usually do it when they're in love. It's a special way to feel close to someone without it becoming sexual."

"Like when you want to be a lady?"

"Yes, exactly like that."

I tapped the remote to resume the movie, and Juliette watched the two actors engage in a long, passionate kiss.

"Does it feel good to kiss?" Juliette asked. "Cary Grant and Deborah Kerr certainly look like they're enjoying it."

I paused the movie again and peered over at Juliette.

"Have you never been kissed? It can be quite pleasurable —if it's done properly."

"So far, my clients have only been interested using my mouth for *other* purposes. Can you show me how it's done properly?"

I smiled at Juliette and placed the remote on the side table.

"It would be my pleasure, Juliette."

I leaned closer to Juliette and placed my lips gently against hers. Her lips were soft and pliable, like the rest of her skin. I closed my eyes and placed my hand behind her neck then turned my head and opened my mouth. When I opened my eyes briefly to see Juliette's reaction, her eyes were wide open. I pulled back, raising my eyebrows.

"You're supposed to close your eyes when you kiss someone," I said. "It's kind of rude to stare at your partner while she's kissing you."

"Really?" Juliette said. "But I was enjoying watching your reaction as you kissed me. I could hear your heart beating faster and feel your breath pulsing on my face."

"Well, yes—those are natural things that happen when someone is enjoying the act, but you're supposed to lose yourself in the kiss, not clinically analyze how your partner is responding to it."

"Like the actors in the movie?"

"Yes."

"But in the movie, their lips were closed the whole time. Your mouth was open—"

"That movie was made more than fifty years ago. The morals of the day were different back then. People weren't supposed to act so...*explicit* in public. Nowadays it's more acceptable to be more expressive and involve a little tongue—"

"Tongue?" Juliette said, with a puzzled expression. "I thought those were meant for other purposes. How does that work?"

"Let me show you. Now shut up and let me kiss you!"

I placed my lips on Juliette's and opened my mouth, inserting my tongue gently into her cavity. I traced it along the inside of her lips, then swirled it around her tongue. She moved her jaw up and down awkwardly, pursing her lips like she'd seen in the movie, but her tongue remained stationary. I pulled back and looked at her again for a moment.

"You *can* move your tongue, can't you?"

"Yes, of course. My clients like it when I—"

"Well, when you're kissing somebody, it's polite and good form to return their actions with somewhat similar actions. You don't want to just sit there and let me do all the work. Good kissing is a two-way exercise."

"Exercise?"

"It's not like lifting weights, silly. Just follow my lead and do what I do."

I leaned back in and resumed kissing Juliette, and this time her tongue became animated as it swirled and played with mine. It was moist and pliable, just like a real tongue. The lubrication didn't feel or taste like regular saliva—it was more innocuous, like water. But Juliette soon got the hang of it, and before long, we were kissing like passionate lovers. I could feel my pussy dampening the more I lost myself in the kiss, and when I opened my eyes this time, Juliette's were closed. After a few minutes, I pulled back and touched her face softly.

"You're a good kisser, Juliette," I said. "And a quick study."

"Study?"

"That means someone who's a good student and learns quickly."

"Teach me what else you like to do, Jade," Juliette said. "I like making you feel good."

I darted my eyes back and forth between each of Juliette's, trying to read her face.

"Does it feel good for you too?" I said.

"I don't feel sensations in the same way that you do. But I can sense what feels good for my clients and I'm programmed to experience this as a positive outcome. The happier I make you, the happier I feel."

"Do you feel happy now?" I asked, peering into her eyes.

"Yes, Jade. You make me very happy. I want you to teach me other ways I can please you."

"Well, I can think of a few other ways you might be able to make me...happy. Would you like to go upstairs to my bedroom now?"

"Yes. I want to feel even closer to you. But will I still be a lady?"

"Yes, Juliette. You'll always be a lady to me."

I stood up off the sofa and reached out my hand to Juliette.

"Come, I want to get closer to you also."

As I led Juliette up the stairs, I could feel my heart pounding in my chest in anticipation of feeling her touch elsewhere on my body. By the time I reached the upper landing, I realized that I'd developed a giant wet spot in the crotch of my jeans. I led her into my bedroom and paused by the foot of my bed, then slowly began to unbutton her blouse. Her large breasts swayed softly on her chest as I separated the two halves, and I leaned in and began to suck on her soft nipples.

"Does it feel good when you kiss my *nipples* too?" Juliette said.

"Yes, very much," I said. "I just wish you could enjoy it as much as I do."

"My pleasure sensors are closely synchronized with yours. The better you feel, the better I feel. I'm enjoying you kissing my breasts."

"Let's see if there are some other places you like being kissed," I said, bending over to unclasp her skirt. When I opened it, I saw that Juliette wasn't wearing any panties. Normally, that would have been a turn-on, but there was something cold about the way that the NextGen staff had dressed her that I found too impersonal. I let her skirt fall to the floor and sat Juliette on the edge of my bed while I removed her shoes. Then I pulled back the covers and asked her to lie down while I removed my own clothes. As she peered up at me, blinking softly with her opalescent eyes, she looked so fragile and innocent.

Jesus, I thought. *This is like taking candy from a baby.*

It felt like I was taking advantage of her, and I paused.

"Are you sure you want to do this?" I said. "I don't want you to feel that I'm...*using* you. I want you to enjoy this as much as I do."

Juliette looked up at me and smiled.

"I've grown quite fond of you in our short time together, Jade. You're the only client who's ever made me feel like a— lady. I want to make love to you."

When Juliette spoke those words, I practically ripped off my clothes and tumbled into the bed beside her.

"Listen," I said, holding my nose close to hers as I peered into her eyes. "Don't ever think of me as a 'client' again. We're friends remember?"

"And now we'll be lovers," Juliette said.

5

CYBER DREAMS

I wrapped my body around Juliette's, feeling her warm skin touching mine. It felt good to give her some tender attention, knowing how she'd been abused by previous NextGen customers. Even though I knew she wasn't real, her innocent human-like responses to my questions and actions had endeared her to me in the short time we'd been together. She was almost like a child, with a blank slate that was rapidly learning and developing her own personality.

"I want you to tell me what you like and everything you feel," I said, gazing into her pretty eyes. "Even if you can't feel things in the same way I do, I sense that you know when something is right or wrong. I think you have feelings in the emotional sense of the word, and I want to focus on making you happy."

Juliette smiled as she blinked at me.

"I enjoy being close to you, Jade. I like the feeling of your body against mine. And I'm happy that you want to be close to me also."

I cradled Juliette's head in my hands and kissed her

softly. Her eyelids closed, and she pushed her body against mine. When she pressed my lips apart with her soft tongue, I moaned. Suddenly she pulled her head back and looked at me with wide eyes.

"Are you alright?" she said. "Did I hurt you?"

"No, silly," I smiled. "When I moan like that, it means you're making me feel good—very good. Please don't stop."

Juliette resumed kissing me, and we intertwined our tongues in a passionate kiss. Her lips felt soft and pliable against mine. If it weren't for the repetitive nature of her motions, I'd be hard-pressed to know it wasn't a real person.

I pulled back and looked at her again.

"I like the way you kiss me, Juliette. But try to mix it up every now and then. We humans like variety in our love-making. If you keep cycling through the same technique over and over, it begins to feel mechanical. Listen to my feedback. That will tell you what's working and what's not."

Juliette looked at me and smiled.

"Thank you for helping me learn to be a better lover, Jade," she said. "I don't want to be so...mechanical. I want to learn how to behave like a real human."

"Just kiss me, beautiful. I'll let you know when you're getting it right."

Juliette placed her lips back on mine, but this time she traced a soft line under my top lip with her tongue, like I'd done to her during the movie. I moaned softly and nodded my head in approval. When she pressed her breasts against mine, I moaned louder, enjoying the feeling of her big tits rubbing against mine. Sensing I wanted fuller body contact, she shifted her weight and rolled on top of me. When I felt her pubis touching mine, I took a deep breath in.

"Yes, Juliette," I said. "That feels good. I like the feeling of your body touching mine."

"Would you like me to touch you in other areas?" she asked with a sly smile.

"Yes. Touch me everywhere. I want to feel your lips and your tongue all over my body."

Juliette raised herself up on her arms and began kissing me softly down the front of my body. When she kissed my neck, I tilted my head and murmured in approval. As she moved past my breasts, I reached out and stopped her head, then gently redirected her face to my breast. I rolled her lips over my nipple and when she extended her wet tongue, I moaned softly.

"Yes, Juliette. Kiss my nipples like you were kissing my mouth. Play with them with your tongue. Lick and suck them like a little lollypop."

Juliette pursed her lips over my nipple, then began running her tongue around the perimeter with her tongue.

"Oh yes," I said. "Just like that."

I could feel my nipple becoming firm as it pressed deeper into her mouth.

Juliette lifted her face off my breast and looked up at me.

"It's getting bigger," she said. "Is that a good thing?"

"Yes," I said. "When you stimulate certain parts of me in the right way, that increases the blood circulation to the area, making it swell. That's definitely a good thing. That means you're making me feel very good. Don't stop."

Juliette resumed sucking and tweaking my nipple with her tongue until it almost became blue from her constant attention.

"Try the *other* one now," I said, tilting my head up. "Remember to mix it up. You never want to stay in any one area doing the same thing for too long."

"I understand," Juliette said.

She moved her face to my other nipple and applied a

similar technique, and I moaned and pressed my breast into her face, signaling my approval. After a minute or two, she lifted her face and looked at me again.

"Is that enough attention on your breasts?" she asked. "Shall I move on to another part of your body so you're not bored?"

I lifted my face and smiled at Juliette.

"I'm far from bored. You're doing a wonderful job. But yes, I'd love to feel your lips on...*other* parts of my body."

Juliette continued kissing my abdomen down the front of my stomach until she got to my mound. Suddenly, she lifted her head and looked at my bare pubis, tilting her head.

"You don't have any hair there, like many of my sibling robots. It's as smooth as the rest of your skin. Are you sure you're a real human?"

I raised myself up into a sitting position and laughed, then kissed Juliette hard on her lips.

"Funny girl. You're developing quite the sense of humor. How do I know *you're* not a real human?

"Well you've seen me when I'm not animated, so I guess that gives it away. But you're always animated, so it's kind of obvious."

"Not always," I said. "We have to sleep just like you sometimes. You'll see a little later. Speaking of which, how are you doing for power supply? I'd hate for you to run out of energy just when things are getting interesting."

Juliette paused to access her power management function.

"I'm still at forty-eight percent of full charge. At my present consumption level, I should last about two more hours before I'll need to recharge."

"Well then, we'd better get busy. We've barely got started learning how to please one another."

Juliette smiled as I leaned back down on the mattress.

"Yes," she said. "I was just about to get to the interesting parts."

She moved down to the foot of my bed and separated my feet about a shoulder width apart. When she began licking my toes, running her tongue into the gap between each one, I giggled.

"Mmm, that feels nice," I said. "Most people don't like to do that. Maybe it's a good thing you can't taste things after all."

"Why don't they like to lick your feet? I thought it felt good to be licked everywhere."

I chuckled at Juliette's naivety.

"Well, yes, that's mostly true. It's just that some people's feet can be pretty smelly and dirty. It's not the cleanest place to put your tongue. But for many of us, our feet is one of our most erogenous zones. It can be especially relaxing to have them massaged with your hands."

Juliette lifted her face from my feet and placed her hands around the arch of my right foot.

"Like this?" she said.

She began squeezing my foot firmly, applying repeating pressure over the top of my foot. I pulled it back, wincing in pain.

"Not so firmly, and not always in the same place," I said. "Use the tips of your fingers to apply gentle pressure, and move your hand around periodically to give my entire foot an even massage."

Juliette softened her grip, and after a few more minutes of my providing verbal guidance, she was giving me a foot massage as good as any professional.

"If you keep learning how to please me this well, I'm going to have a hard time returning you," I purred.

Juliette paused and looked at me, processing what I'd just said. Her expression almost looked like I'd hurt her with the suggestion that I wouldn't need her again soon.

"Shall I move on to your other foot now?" she said. "Like I did with your breasts earlier? I don't want you to get bored with me..."

Suddenly, my heart began racing and I my pussy pulsed, as I felt myself drawing closer to Juliette. I wanted to feel her lips in my most sensitive place and show her how much I needed her.

"You could never bore me, Juliette," I said, pulling myself up again. "In fact, you're the most fascinating person I've met in a very long time. Why don't you do my other foot another time? Right now, there's some parts of me closer to my core that are getting all warm and fuzzy."

I spread my legs further apart and swiveled my hips to direct her attention further up my body.

"Touch me between my legs. I want to show you how happy you really make me."

Juliette lowered her face to my foot again and began kissing her way softly up my leg. The higher she moved, the wider I spread my legs, until her face lay directly in front of my steaming box.

"Kiss me there, Juliette," I said. "Kiss me in my most sensitive spot."

She repositioned herself between my outstretched legs then lowered her face to my pussy. When I felt her lips touch my wet labia, I gasped.

"Yes, baby," I moaned. "Right there. Lick my slit. Kiss me like you did earlier."

Juliette inserted her tongue into my hole and began

tracing it along the inside of my lips toward my clit. When she reached my nub, I let out a deep guttural moan.

"Yes," I panted. "Suck my clit, Juliette. It feels so good."

Juliette took my button into her mouth and began circling it with her tongue as she'd done with my mouth earlier. I lifted my hips and pressed my pussy harder against her face. In a way, it felt even better having Juliette touch me there than a real person. Whether it was just the insane idea of having the ultimate sex machine administering to me in the most intimate way, or it was her rapidly improving technique, I couldn't be sure. Either way, I found myself getting lost in the experience as my pussy buzzed in delirious excitement.

As I pressed my pussy harder against her face signaling for her to continue, she pursed her lips around the tip of my clit and sucked it into her mouth.

"Fuck, yes!" I moaned. "Just like that, baby. Don't stop. Keep sucking me just like that."

Juliette suddenly lifted her face and looked at me strangely.

"But I thought you said you wanted me to mix it up after a while? Don't you want me to move on to another body part now?"

"God, no!" I panted. "This particular body part is different from the rest. Once you get the right technique going, I don't want you to stop. This specific part needs a certain amount of consistent stimulation in order to reach the peak of pleasure."

"How will I know when you get there? With my male clients I can always tell when they want me to stop because—"

"I'll let you know," I said. "Right now, I just want you to keep doing what you were doing. It feels really good."

Juliette smiled, then lowered her head and placed her lips back around my button. As she began swirling her lips around my organ, I moaned out loud, encouraging her to continue. She alternated between licking and sucking my jewel, and as my passion continued to rise, I began to feel the rising tide of my climax approaching.

"Place your fingers inside me now, honey," I panted. "I want you to feel me cumming in your hand. I'm close, baby. Don't stop."

Juliette inserted the middle and forefinger of her right hand into my slit, and I shifted my hips down until her knuckles pressed hard against my opening.

"Uhnn!" I groaned. "Yes, that feels so good, Juliette! Fuck me with your fingers while you suck my love button. I'm going to cum all over you soon."

When Juliette began thrusting her fingers in and out of my snatch and bending them so the tips rubbed against my G-spot, my climax quickly washed over me.

"Yes, Juliette!" I screamed. "I'm cumming! Feel me cumming on your face and fingers. Oh—Goddd!"

As my pussy clamped down over Juliette's fingers, I suddenly gushed the huge build-up of lubrication inside my pussy all over her sweet face, in a series of long hard spurts. I placed my hands behind her face in fear that she might think something was wrong and stop touching me at the worst possible time. My powerful contractions continued for almost a full minute as I writhed and moaned like a wounded animal on my bed. When the contractions finally stopped, I flung my arms to the side of my body and collapsed, exhausted onto the bed.

Juliette lifted her dripping face from my pussy and looked up at me innocently.

"Did you like that, Jade? Did I make you happy?"

I lifted myself back up into a sitting position and placed my hands beside her head, pulling her close to me. I kissed her passionately, swirling my tongue inside her mouth, tasting my juices inside her.

"Yes, sweetie," I said, pulling back and peering into her eyes. "You've made me very happy. You're a very good student."

"And you're a good teacher," she smiled. "I want to learn everything I can from you so I can become real lady."

I held Juliette's face in my hands again and kissed her all over her face. She no longer felt or seemed at all like a robot to me. She just seemed like a sweet, new...lover."

"You're already more of a lady than ninety-nine percent of the real humans I know," I said. "I feel very...close to you. Now I want to make *you* feel happy. Lie down while I return the favor. I want to touch and taste you everywhere also."

Juliette paused as she pinched her eyebrows together.

"But...I can't experience pleasure and sexual climax like you can. Most of my clients only want to—"

"I'm not one of your clients, remember? We're friends now, lovers. Let me at least pretend to give you pleasure. Concentrate on what I'm doing and think about how it made me feel when you did these things to me. You said that it makes you feel happy when you know you're making me feel happy. Channel those happy thoughts while I make love your body."

"Yes, Jade," Juliette said. "I think I know what you mean. Make love to me. I want to know what it's like for a real woman to feel pleasure like you do."

"Lie back then and just relax. Talk to me like I did when you sense or remember something I'm doing as feeling pleasurable. Feel me...loving you."

"Yes, Jade. I want to feel your love."

I placed my arm behind Juliette's back and gently lowered her onto the bed, then I lay on top of her and kissed her softly.

"You're beautiful, Juliette," I said. "In every possible way. I love..." I paused, stopping myself from saying the unthinkable. "Making love to you."

As I continued kissing Juliette, rolling my tongue inside her mouth, she began to moan softly. My pussy pulsed again, and I felt a dribble of lubrication leak down over our thighs.

"Do you like that, sweetie?" I asked, lifting my head and peering into her eyes.

"Yes," Juliette said. "Please don't stop."

My mouth stretched into a wide grin and I lowered my head to her lips again. I kissed her for many long minutes, savoring the texture and moisture of her mouth, running my tongue between her lips and her teeth, probing every square inch of her. Juliette moaned and purred in approval with each adjustment of my lips and tongue as she pressed her mouth firmly against mine.

I could have kissed her all night long, but I was eager to feel and taste the rest of her. After a few minutes, I raised myself up and began kissing my way down her body. When I got to her plump breasts, I squeezed them between my hands, marveling at how realistic they felt. Unlike other fake boobs I'd felt, these had a natural shape to them and they moved freely on her chest like real breasts.

"You have magnificent breasts," I said, staring at her melons like I'd never seen bare tits before.

"Thank you, Jade. I like yours too."

Part of me wanted to just squeeze and play with her stack for the rest of the night, I was so enamored with them. I'd always fantasized about making love to Christina

Fredricks with her full figure, and here lay her buxom avatar directly underneath me. But I was mindful of treating her like a sex toy, realizing that most of the men she'd been with had probably fixated excessively on her tits.

I leaned down and took one of her nipples into my mouth and sucked on it gently. After a few seconds, it seemed to grow bigger and I lifted my head up, noticing that they'd expanded almost to the size of the end in my pinky finger.

"Your body parts get bigger and harder too," I said, opening my eyes wide. "It looks like I'm not the *only* one who enjoys a good licking every now and then."

"My body's physiognomy is programmed to respond just like a real woman's," Juliette said. "It makes for a more realistic sexual experience."

"Well, you just lie back and let your program learn to *feel* like a real woman also. I'm going to make love to you like you've never experienced it before."

I lowered my head back onto Juliette's nipple and sucked and flicked her appendage inside my mouth. It was firm, but soft and bendable. It even had a small dimple in the center, like a real nipple.

If this is how authentic they make all of her body parts, no wonder she's so popular, I thought.

After a few minutes, I refocused my attention to her other breast, changing up my technique periodically in an effort to keep her amused.

"I like how you mix it up, Jade," she said. "You're a very skilled lover."

"Thank you, Juliette. I might have had a little more practice than you. But I want you to tell me whenever I'm getting boring or monotonous. We can *all* learn to become better lovers."

I continued sucking and teasing Juliette's nipples for a little longer, then I kissed my way down her abdomen and stopped at her belly button. I placed my ear to her tummy and heard a gentle hum emanating from her midsection.

"Is that your CPU I hear?" I said, looking up at her.

"That's actually my battery pack," she said. "There's a small fan in there to keep everything from overheating. My CPU is in my head, just like regular people."

I chuckled at Juliette's human comparison.

"Where does all your heat go?" I asked. "Most computers have some kind of vent to discharge their internal heat..."

"You might be surprised to learn that I vent out of my anus. When it's not otherwise in use, there's a little internal flap that opens to discharge excessive heat."

My eyes opened in wonder as I laughed out loud.

"What? You actually *fart* like real people too? It sounds like you *do* void after all!"

"Maybe a little," Juliette said, and we both giggled together for a moment.

"Just don't fart when I'm down there, okay?" I said. "Because that's considered bad form."

"Don't worry, my designers figured that all out. I only vent when I'm not in use."

"Well that's good, because I still had a little more use in mind for you."

I separated Juliette's legs gently, then lowered myself beneath her and pressed my face toward her crotch. When I was a few inches from her opening, I paused to look at her genitals. Just like a regular woman, she had two sets of labia joining at the top to form a gentle bump where a fold of flesh rested over her faux clitoris. I could see the head peeking out from under the hood, like a little round pearl.

Holy crap, I thought. *Juliette's right. Her designers didn't miss a single detail when they crafted her.*

Her entire vulva, from her soft mound down to her little pink rosebud, was perfectly formed and symmetrical. If Juliette was correct about symmetry being one of the defining features of beauty, then she couldn't have been a more perfect and gorgeous specimen.

I reached out my hand and ran my fingers along her inner lips, feeling a slippery, translucent film. I raised my fingers to my mouth and tasted her lubrication. It had a pleasing taste and smell, with a faint citrus aroma.

Incredible, I thought. *She even tastes like the ideal woman.*

I lowered my head and started licking Juliette from the base of her slit toward the top. As she squeezed her buttocks, she moaned softly. I placed my hands under her cheeks and felt her ass quivering as I continued kissing and sucking her.

"That's my girl," I said. "Show me what you like."

Whether she was simply mimicking my movements from when she went down on me earlier, or she was trying to signal what she was truly feeling, was unclear. Either way, it was turning me on tremendously, and I pressed my pussy into the mattress in sympathy with her.

When my tongue reached her clit and began circling it in a slow arc, Juliette moaned, raising her hips off the bed. As I began sucking her button in and out of my mouth, she rocked her hips, pressing her pussy more firmly into my mouth.

"Yes," I murmured into her pussy. "Do you like that, baby?"

"Yes, Jade," Juliette moaned. "My pleasure receptors are firing like crazy."

"Mmm," I hummed into her soft cunny. "Let it go, baby. Let yourself feel everything I'm doing to you."

As her clit hardened and extended further into my mouth, I sucked on it harder, tracing figure eights around her nub with my tongue.

"Yes," Juliette purred. "Whatever you're doing, keep going. It feels good."

As she began to rock her pussy faster and harder against my mouth, she raised her hips off the bed again, and I inserted three fingers into her box. Her pussy was warm and tight inside, and it pulsed gently against my fingers as she raised and lowered her hips.

"Yes, Jade," Juliette moaned. "Fuck me with your fingers. I like feeling you inside me."

Whether she'd been programmed to talk dirty when having sex with her partners or had picked it up from me, I wasn't sure. But when she said that, my own pussy suddenly pulsed with desire and I began to grind my mound into the mattress trying to stimulate my tingling clit. I wasn't sure if it was all an act or she was just mimicking what I had done, but I was determined to see how far I could take her. I pressed my fingers deep inside her pussy and began curling my fingers against the front wall of her cavern.

"Yes, Jade!" Juliette moaned louder. "Touch me there. That feels so good. I want to cum in your mouth, Jade. Make me cum like a real woman."

I pressed my fingers more firmly against her G-spot while I increased the speed of my tongue action around her clit. I could feel her button throbbing in my mouth and the walls of her pussy closing down on my hand. Suddenly, Juliette lifted her hips high off the bed and shouted my name.

"Jade!" she screamed. "I'm cumming! Kiss me! Kiss me with your soft, sweet lips!"

I could feel Juliette's lubrication dripping down my hand as I continued thrusting my fingers into her pussy, feeling her nub twisting in my mouth. Even her vagina seemed to pulse against my fingers, as if she was experiencing real contractions from a climax. If this wasn't the real thing, I thought, it was certainly the most convincing fake orgasm that I'd ever witnessed.

When she finally stopped shaking and moaning, I pulled myself up and lay down beside her. I looked into her eyes and noticed that her pupils were still dilated.

"Did you enjoy that, sweetie?" I asked.

"Yes, Jade. Thank you for loving me so tenderly. No one has ever been able to make me feel like that before."

As I lay beside her listening to her soft hum, I began to wonder how I'd ever be able to part ways with my new best friend.

6

———

BEST FRIENDS

After we made love, Juliette and I cuddled in bed for a while talking about her experiences and aspirations. She asked me just as many questions about my own life experiences and dreams, and the more we talked, the more I found myself drawn to her. It was strange to have such strong feelings for something I knew wasn't real, but I found her innocent sense of wonder absolutely irresistible.

The more I thought about it, her responses to the world around her and her development as a caring, intelligent being wasn't so different from real humans. It was a shame that her previous customers had only been interested in having sex with her, because she had so much more to offer. If humans were truly separated from other animals by their unique ability to feel empathy and other social emotions, she seemed more human to me than many of the real people I knew.

As we approached midnight, Juliette informed me that her battery power was almost fully depleted, and she showed me how to recharge her. I watched in amazement as she placed two hands beside her belly button and stretched the skin apart. Then she reached inside and pulled out a cord with a standard electric plug. I found a long extension cord, and after plugging her into the nearest wall outlet, we fell asleep in each other's arms.

In the morning, I filled a bubble bath and we giggled and teased each other as we flicked the soft suds at each other. After a half hour or so, the front doorbell rang and I put on a robe and walked downstairs to see who it was. When I peered through the view hole, I was surprised to see my best friend, Hannah. I opened the door partway and stuck my head out, blocking the entrance.

"Where've you been?" she asked, in an irritated voice. "I've been calling you nonstop for the past twenty-four hours and you haven't picked up."

"I've just been kind of busy lately," I said. "Can we get caught up later tomorrow? I've got a lot going on right now."

Hannah peered at me with a confused expression as she tilted her head, trying to look into my house.

"Aren't you going to invite me inside? It's not like I haven't seen you in a bathrobe before."

I didn't want to have to explain why I didn't feel comfortable inviting her into my house, but I knew I had to provide a good excuse to make her go away.

"Sorry, I've got company..."

"Oh?" she said, a sneer forming on her face. "Is it that pretty neighbor girl you were telling me about a few weeks ago? I'd love to meet her sometime—"

Suddenly Hannah's eyes grew wide as saucers as her focus shifted to some movement behind me. I heard footsteps approaching and turned around to see Juliette standing totally naked in the hallway, dripping sudsy water onto the floor.

"Is everything alright, Jade?" she asked. "I heard some excited voices and was worried about you."

Hannah's eyes widened in amazement as she took in all of Juliette's sexy naked figure.

"Holy shit!" she said. "Now I see why you didn't want to invite me inside. Aren't you going to introduce me to your friend?"

I glanced to the left and right to see if any neighbors were watching, then I quickly escorted Hannah inside.

"Hannah," I said motioning to the stark naked robot, "this is Juliette. Juliette, this is my friend Hannah."

"Oh goody!" Juliette said, clapping her hands together. "I've never met a client's friend before. Tell me all about her. I want to know everything about you."

Hannah's eyebrows pinched together in a confused expression as she looked at Juliette for a long moment, then she turned to me.

"*Client*?" she said. "Who exactly *is* this person? And why does she sound so strange?"

"She's just a—business associate."

Hannah looked back at Juliette standing dripping wet and motionless on the floor, then her eyes suddenly flew wide open.

"Is this one of those sophisticated new *sex robots* I've been reading about?"

She stepped forward and poked Juliette gently in the shoulder and Juliette didn't move.

"Oh my God, Jade! She's magnificent! Is she fully...*functional*?"

Hannah reached out and squeezed Juliette's large breasts, then her hand moved down between her legs.

I quickly stepped forward and swiped Hannah's hand away from Juliette's body.

"What the fuck, Hannah!" I said. "Show a little respect. She's not just a toy for you to play with."

Hannah looked at me dumbfounded for a moment, then peered back at Juliette, leering at her body.

"Ah—*yeah*," she said, cocking her head sarcastically. "That's *exactly* what she is. Don't tell me you haven't been *playing* with your little sex toy all this time."

"She's so much more than just a...*robot*," I said. "We've really gotten to know one another over the last day or so, and I've grown quite fond of her."

"Yes, I can see why," Hannah said, running her eyes up and down Juliette's buxom body. "Why don't you show me everything she can do? I wouldn't mind getting a piece of this action too."

As she stepped forward and began lasciviously caressing Juliette's body, I stepped between them and pushed Hannah toward the door.

"Don't *touch* her!" I yelled. "She's already been plenty abused by other people. I think it's time you left now."

Hannah shook her head and looked at me in shock.

"Are you kidding me? I'm your best friend, for fuck's sake. Aren't you going to share this incredible specimen with me? Don't you remember our last camping trip—"

"It's not like that," I said. "Juliette is different. That was just us girls having fun. This one is...special."

Hannah furrowed her eyebrows and looked at me dumbfounded.

"Are you listening to yourself? She's a *robot*! A glorified sex doll. You can't actually be developing *feelings* for this thing?"

"You wouldn't understand," I said, pushing Hannah toward the front entrance. "I'll talk to you tomorrow. Right now, I want you to leave."

I escorted Hannah outside, then closed and locked the door behind her.

"I'm so sorry for that," I said, turning toward Juliette, wrapping my arms around her. "Let's get you dried off and presentable."

"Is that true what you said to your friend Hannah?" she said. "That I'm...special? And that you're developing feelings toward me?"

I paused for a moment, peering into Juliette's limpid eyes, then I sighed.

"Yes," I said. "I've grown quite close to you in the short time we've been together."

Juliette turned her head as she listened to Hannah's car exit my driveway.

"Am I your...best friend now?"

"You're so much more than just a friend to me, Juliette," I said, kissing her softly.

As we intertwined our tongues together in another passionate kiss, Juliette pressed her wet mound against my robe, and I felt my pussy begin to dampen inside.

"Come," Juliette said, clasping my hand in hers and pulling me toward the stairs. "We haven't got much more time together. I want to feel you close to me for every remaining second."

We tumbled into bed and wrapped our arms and legs around one another, writhing and grinding our hips together. I lay down near Juliette's feet and pulled my body toward her until our pussies touched. When I straddled her hips with my legs and began scissoring our clits together, she lifted her head and looked up at me with a puzzled expression.

"What's this technique?" she said. "I've never experienced this type of sexual activity before."

I paused for a moment with my button buzzing between my legs.

"It's something two women do when they want to make love together. We rub out most sensitive parts together and make each other feel good."

"But I can't *see* you down there. I want to look into your eyes and watch your face while I give you pleasure."

I lifted myself up and smiled at Juliette.

"Yes, you're right. It's always better when we can watch each other."

I positioned myself on top of her and placed my mound against hers, lowering my face to her lips. As we began to kiss, we tilted our hips until our clits touched, and I moaned in Juliette's mouth. I opened my eyes for a moment and saw that she was looking at me as we made love to one another. But this time I didn't mind. While we kissed and ground our bodies together, our passion grew in a rising crescendo, until we both screamed in ecstasy at the intense pleasure we'd given one another. As I shook and panted atop Juliette, coming down from my climax, she held me softly and peered into my eyes.

"I don't want to leave you, Jade," she said.

"I don't want you to leave either," I said, kissing her softly on her cheek.

I lay down beside her and closed my eyes, shaking my head.

How could I go back to the real thing when I already held the perfect woman in my arms?

Feeling the burn never felt so good...

Everyone's an exhibitionist in disguise...

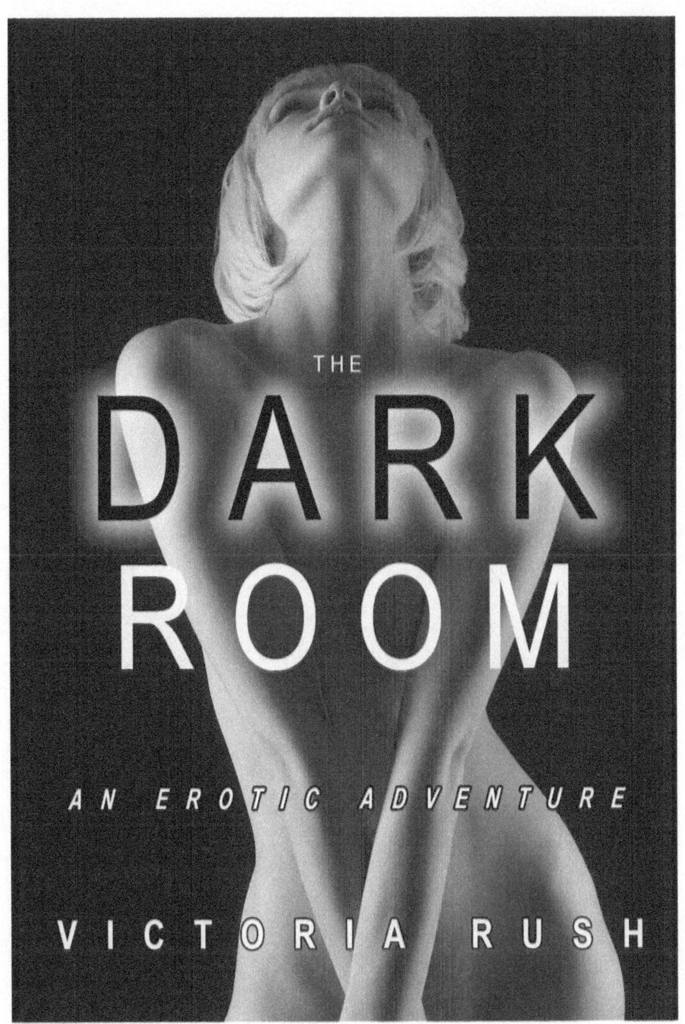

Everything's sexier in the dark...

NAKED YOGA

AN EROTIC ADVENTURE

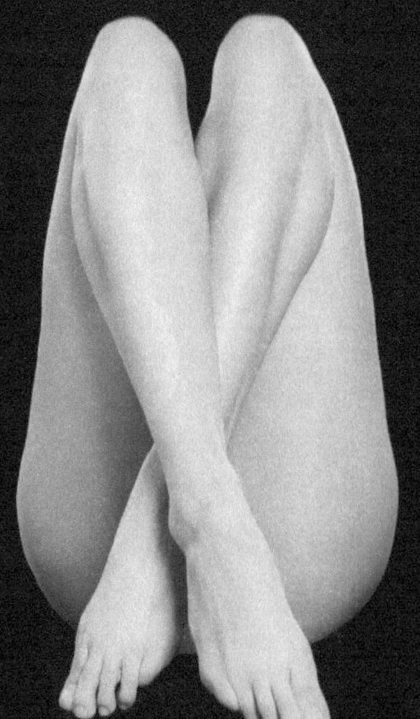

VICTORIA RUSH

Mula Bandha is for lovers...

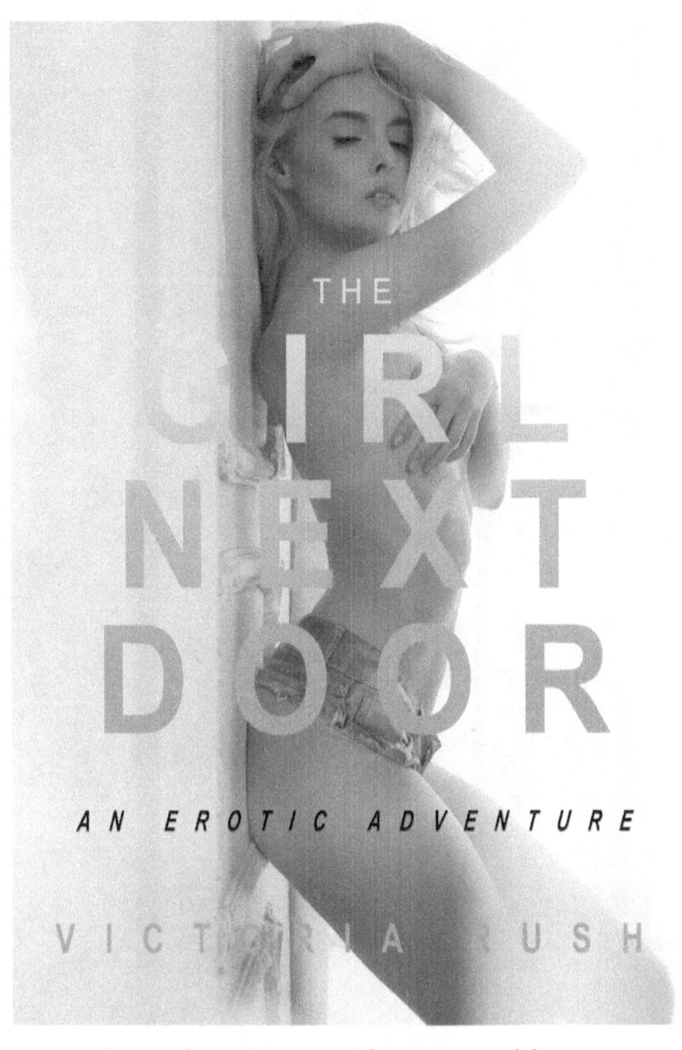

Some people can get into pretty tight spots on a crowded train...

Jade's EROTIC ADVENTURES

BOOKS 1 - 5

VICTORIA RUTH

The complete five-book bestselling series — 60% off

THE DINNER PARTY - PREVIEW
FINGER FOOD

Sometime later, I heard a soft tap on my bedroom door. Not wanting to remove myself just yet from my cocoon of luxury, I called out to answer.

"Yes?"

"It's time for your massage," a woman's voice replied.

"Just one minute please."

I reluctantly stepped out of the bath and quickly toweled myself dry. I wrapped a large bath sheet around me, re-donned my mask, then opened the bedroom door.

A petite young Asian girl greeted me, wearing a kimono similar to mine and a crimson masquerade mask.

Apparently not everybody who works here always walks around stark naked.

The girl was utterly breathtaking. Long jet-black hair cascaded over high cheekbones past pouty lips, her delicate collarbones peeking from the top of her kimono. I could see her breasts and hips outlined by the tightly-wrapped kimono and suddenly wished that she too had come to my boudoir naked.

"My name is Jasmine," she said. "I'm your personal

masseuse and esthetician. Are you ready for your final preparation?

Just the thought of this beauty laying her tender hands on me sent a shiver down my spine.

"Definitely. Please come in. How would you like me to prepare?"

"Come with me, please."

Jasmine led me into the bathroom, where she nonchalantly removed her kimono and hung it behind the bathroom door.

Oh my God.

I didn't think anyone in this place could get more beautiful or sensuous. Jasmine had perfectly shaped B-cup breasts with a thin indentation running down the center of her perfectly toned stomach. Like everyone else in this place, her pubis was utterly bald and flawless. She barely looked eighteen and I was just about to ask her age, but she spoke first.

"If you'd like to remove your towel and lay face down on the table, we can get started. May I call you Jade?"

There was something about her confident manner and tone that belied her youthful appearance. I had no inhibitions whatsoever about displaying myself unclothed to this stranger.

"Yes, thank you, Jasmine." I unhooked my bath sheet and threw it against the side of the tub.

"Would you like me to drape your backside?" Jasmine asked.

"That won't be necessary," I quickly answered.

Jasmine walked over to the vanity counter and picked up two small bottles of oil resting under an orange radiant lamp. She brought them back to the massage table, opened one, and poured the oil into one cupped hand then rubbed her hands together. The scent of lavender wafted toward my nose.

I closed my eyes in anticipation of her touch. I'd had massages before, but nothing as sensuous and stimulating as this. When her hands touched the small of my back, I jerked reflexively from the sexual tension. My heart was beating a hundred miles an hour as I felt the blood coursing through my veins.

Jasmine must have sensed my nervous tension and began pressing her fingers more firmly into my back as she moved them slowly up each side of my spine. The warm oil allowed her hands to glide effortlessly across my skin. She used every surface of her hands to massage my muscles, expertly kneading my skin with her fingers and palm.

I began to relax as my muscles softened and surrendered to her touch. She sensuously massaged every part of my back, shoulders, and neck, applying just the right amount of pressure. Periodically, she would pour more warm oil on my lower back, dipping her hands in it to replenish the silky lubrication against my pliant skin.

Just as the sexual tension began to subside from the utter relaxation of the massage, Jasmine moved her hands down to my buttocks and began to caress them in soft circular motions. My glutes contracted involuntarily and I unconsciously pressed my mound into the firm padding of the table. Suddenly I was quickly reminded that a gorgeous young woman was caressing my naked body. She cupped each buttock between her hands as she massaged my ass tantalizingly, her little finger sliding slowly into the cleft just above my anus.

Periodically, I'd partially open one of my eyes with my head turned in her direction to look at her gorgeous body. My head was at the same level as her midsection, and my mouth watered as I watched her stomach muscles flex and her hips undulate with each movement of her hands. At times her pussy was almost right beside me and I wanted to reach out and run my own fingers up her soft legs.

I was in total heaven and getting wetter by the moment. Just when I thought I couldn't stand it anymore, she suddenly moved her hands down to my feet and began massaging her thumbs into my soles.

I'd always loved having my feet massaged, but nobody did it like Jasmine. She cradled my foot and used every part of her hands to massage and knead every surface from my heel to my toes. I didn't want her to stop, but there were other parts of my body that were screaming for attention.

As if reading my thoughts, she began moving her hands up toward my calf, using her thumbs to spread the muscle apart. She lingered almost as long on my calf as she had on my foot, rolling the ball of my calf between both of her hands, sliding her slick hands up and down erotically. I couldn't help imagining how she might use those same hands to massage a man's erect cock in a similar manner. My mind wandered again to what pleasures lay in wait for me over dinner.

After shifting her hands to my right leg and giving my other foot and calf similar attention, she placed each hand just behind my knees and began to slowly move them up towards my buttocks. Her thumbs pressed against my inner thighs as she glided tantalizingly close to my apex.

I rolled my legs outward in an invitation to move closer. My legs were parted enough that I was sure she could see my vulva from her vantage point behind me. In my highly aroused state, my lips were engorged and spread apart, revealing my moist and quivering opening.

But as much as I desperately wanted her to, Jasmine

never touched me there. She repeatedly slid her hands right up to the edge of my slit, pressing and rotating her thumbs on the fleshy meat of my upper thighs just below my aching pussy. I suppose this was part of her master plan—to tease me mercilessly and inflame my passions so I'd be ready for just about anything at the main event.

It was certainly working. After thirty minutes of Jasmine's ministrations, I was grinding my pussy into the table trying desperately to give my clit some needed direct stimulation.

Just when I thought I couldn't be teased any more tanta-lizingly, Jasmine opened one of the bottles of warm oil and poured it directly into the crack of my ass. She paused as the fluid flowed down and directly over my parted lips. I almost came from the gentle movement of the warm liquid as it trickled across the folds of my labia, channeled toward the junction where they joined together at my clit. I shuddered in pleasure at the feeling, even if it was only the subtlest of touch.

Jasmine suddenly interrupted my thoughts.

"Would you like to turn over now?"

It was the first time she had spoken directly to me since the massage started, and it surprised me in my catatonic, pre-orgasmic state. I practically flipped over like a fish out of water and spread my legs expectantly. Finally, I'd get some relief. Surely, she couldn't leave me hanging like this.

"It's time for your final grooming," she said. "I'll need you to part your legs a bit further to provide full access."

Grooming? I knew this was part of the process, but somehow it didn't seem fair to transition at this precise moment. At least I'd be able to stay on the comfortable massage table instead of the clinical vinyl chairs used by my regular esthetician.

Jasmine walked over to another cabinet by the makeup table and withdrew a leather bag from one of the drawers, then brought it back to the table. She reached into the bag and pulled out a cordless hair trimmer.

"Do you have a preference regarding your appearance?" she asked. "Do you prefer natural, neatly trimmed, or bare?"

I knew she was referring to my pubic hair, which I generally kept neatly trimmed. I'd always thought going fully bald was unnatural and unseemly, catering to men's prurient fantasies of fucking young schoolgirls. But in this situation, it seemed entirely appropriate, like I was stripping away all my camouflage and armor.

If tonight was all about being watched, I might as well bare myself in every sense of the word and truly let my inhibitions go. I began to fantasize about rubbing my bare pussy against Jasmine's while she poured warm oil between us. The more work she had to do on me, the more chance I'd have to make this last and hopefully get off.

I didn't hesitate. "Bare, thank you."

"As you wish," she said. "I'll remove the long hairs first with the trimmer, then shave you smooth with a razor."

No waxing? This was different. I was relieved to not have to bear the painful and violent trial of having my hairs ripped out en masse. Although shaving down there was always a scary proposition, I felt safe in the capable and practiced hands of this beautiful esthetician.

Jasmine nodded, then flipped a switch on the trimmer. The device buzzed softly as she placed it gently on my mound. I had only a light dusting of fur and it didn't take long for her to remove it with a few short strokes over my pubis. I shuddered as the vibrations penetrated deep into my core. If she had placed the flat head on my clitoris, I would have popped off in a millisecond. Instead, she turned the trimmer face-down and gently swiped the vibrating teeth against the sides of my vulva, sensuously separating my labia with her hands as she moved the device between my legs to trim the hairs on the inside and outside of my labia.

It was an insanely titillating feeling, but just clinical enough to bring me down from my plateau and shift my focus. My mind wandered to the upcoming feast, and I contemplated what surprises lay in wait at the main event. The hostesses had suggested there would be 'contact' of some sort during the meal, and I was intrigued exactly who and how it would be administered. The idea of being fully bald, cleansed, and thoroughly stimulated going into the event was an incredible rush.

Jasmine continued with the trimmer all the way down my perineum to my anus, barely touching me with the trimmer so as not to pinch any delicate tissues. Apparently there were no parts of my erogenous zone that would remain untouched, now—and perhaps later.

She turned off the trimmer and placed it at the foot of the table. Then she took a bottle of gel from the bag and spread the gel on her hands. Using both hands, she spread it gently between my legs, starting on my mound all the way down to my rosebud.

My body almost levitated above the table as Jasmine finally laid her hands directly on my clitoris. The gel had a mild stinging quality that added to the stimulating sensation. If this was meant to excite my follicles in preparation for the shave, it wasn't the only feature of my anatomy that it made erect. I could feel the hood of my clitoris retract as my button filled with blood and began to push outward. Suddenly, I was fully stimulated again and lusting for Jasmine's touch. I fantasized about her bending down and taking my swollen nub between her puffy lips and letting me come in her mouth.

Unfortunately, my satisfaction would have to wait a little longer. Instead, Jasmine reached into her bag and pulled out a straight-edge razor. In anyone else's hands, it might look threatening, especially in my prostrated and vulnerable position. But something about the way she delicately and sensuously opened the jackknifed tool instantly evaporated my fears. I could see how this type of razor would in fact give her better control safely cutting my stubs instead of the usual ladies plastic razor.

With her right hand, Jasmine gently laid the razor on its flat edge at the top of my mound, while she gently pulled my skin upwards with her other hand. Then she slowly turned the sharp edge perpendicular to my skin and began softly scraping the razor downwards. I could hear the bristling sound as the razor edge removed my nubs right down to the follicles. She repeated the pattern in one inch wide swipes on one side then the other of my pubis, being ever-so-careful to stop just where my clitoris lay quivering in a mixture of fear and excitement. There was something about the utter vulnerability of the procedure that made it the most erotic experience I'd ever had.

Jasmine used the same deft touch as she moved down my vulva and perineum, scraping the vestiges of stray hairs away with gentle swipes of the long blade, while sensuously separating my folds and flesh with her other hand. She took extra time and care around my anus and clit, using the gentlest and slowest motion I've ever felt someone apply to my body. The combination of fright and titillation as she probed my most sensitive body parts created a river of sensuous fluids running down my vulva. By this time, no shaving gel was necessary to provide a smooth gliding surface for the knife.

When she was finished, Jasmine retrieved a fresh wash towel from beside the sink and held it under the warm water faucet then twisted the excess water into the basin. She returned to the table and placed it over my splayed legs then gently cleansed the excess moisture and remaining shaving gel with gentle massaging movements of her hands. The warm, moist towel felt exquisite against my newly shaved skin. Jasmine's hands now felt comforting between my legs rather than erotic.

She had taken me on an incredibly sensuous erotic arc, right to the edge of ecstasy and back, to a quiet relaxed place. I exhaled fully and completely for the first time in almost an hour.

Jasmine removed the towel from between my legs and held up a large hand mirror at a forty-five degree angle toward me.

"What do you think?" she asked.

I tilted my head up and studied her masterpiece. Far from the usual red and swollen vulva that I typically experienced after the violent waxing with my regular esthetician, I'd never seen my pussy look so beautiful. Utterly bereft of any hair, my entire perineum from my pubic mound to my anus was totally bald, pink—and gorgeous. I just stared at my beautiful pussy, utterly transfixed by the transformation.

"You have to *feel* it to really appreciate how beautiful you are, Jade," Jasmine purred.

I moved my right hand down, running my fingers along the edges of my pussy. I gasped from a feeling I'd never felt before. It felt smooth as silk: no bumps or blemishes or cuts or bruises. It was almost as if I was feeling somebody else— somebody I'd never felt before. I couldn't stop my left hand joining the other in rubbing and caressing my sensitive organs.

Jasmine lowered the mirror and smiled at me as I felt the moisture begin to accumulate between my legs again.

"It's almost time for your dinner appointment," she said. "Why don't you save the best for last? I think you'll find plenty of ways to satisfy your appetite over the next couple of hours."

She lifted my kimono from the hook at the edge of the bathtub and held it open for me.

"I'll escort you downstairs now if you're ready. All you need to bring is your kimono and slippers—and your mask of course."

I sat up slowly and stepped off the massage table. Turning around, I held my arms out as Jasmine lifted one arm of the silk robe onto me then the other. Then she turned around to face me, wrapped the silk tie around me, and tied a single bow over my belly button. She retrieved my matching silk slippers and knelt down on one knee to gently lift my feet one at a time and place them softly inside. It took every ounce of my power not to grab her head and pull it into my pulsating pussy.

Jasmine stood up gracefully and smiled into my eyes.

"If you'll follow me, I'll escort you now to the fantasy feast."

She didn't bother putting her own robe on. Her tight little ass barely jiggled as she stepped smartly ahead of me. I wasn't sure if I'd have a chance to feel Jasmine's touch again before the evening was over, but for now I was in total bliss ogling her petite, curvaceous figure from behind...

Read More

ABOUT THE AUTHOR

If you would like to receive notification of new book(s) in Jade's Erotic Adventures, follow me at http://bookbub.com/authors/victoria-rush.

If you have a moment, please post a brief review on my Amazon book page at viewbook.at/sm . Even just a couple of sentences will help other readers find and enjoy this book as much as you hopefully did.

Follow, share, like, and comment at:

www.facebook.com/authorvictoriarush
www.pinterest.com/authorvictoriarush
www.twitter.com/authorvictoriarush
authorvictoriarush@outlook.com

Hope to see you again soon!

www.ingramcontent.com/pod-product-compliance
Lightning Source LLC
Chambersburg PA
CBHW031630130726
47900CB00018B/740